I0620931

the perfect lover spell

A Short Time Travel, Accidental Magic Romance
with HEA

coral cove
book six

Jax Wilder

Rainbow Quartz Publishing

The Perfect Lover Spell© 2024 by Jax Wilder
Rainbow Quartz Publishing

Published by Rainbow Quartz Publishing

RQPublishing.com

RainbowQuartzPublishing@gmail.com

Edmonds, WA 98026

This is a work of fiction. Names, characters, places, and incidents are either the product of the author's imagination or used fictitiously. Any resemblance to actual events, locales, or persons, living or dead, is entirely coincidental.

ISBN: 978-1-961714-50-2

Cover design by Miranda Townsend

Edited by Miranda Townsend

For my witchy kin.
I see you.

jessa

Z eus, in his cruelty, tore humans apart, leaving us fractured and incomplete, destined to roam the earth in search of the missing pieces of our souls.

More specifically, our soulmates.

Most of us stumble through life, swiping left or right, convinced that a filtered selfie of a random stranger might somehow unlock the door to true love. Honestly, it's laughable. I've swiped right more times than I can count, but not one of those digital matches has ever led me to anything resembling love.

Take Mason, for instance. He was a charming ex-Mormon who had a serious grudge against caffeine and a terrifying knack for emotional manipulation. He chipped away at me, slowly eroding my confidence like he had done to countless women before me. But the final nail in the coffin? His blatant homophobia. That was the moment I realized I had absolutely no room in my life for bigots.

Then there was Lawrence. He was suave, sophisticated, and completely married—though he conveniently left out that minor detail. He invited me on what I thought was a romantic moonlit stroll after a party, where we shared secrets and flirtatious banter. That is, until we bumped into his wife, who was casually leaving the same party. Talk about an awkward encounter. Nothing says "run for the hills" like being the unintentional side piece.

Mutton Chops—yes, that's how I remember him—looked like the perfect match on paper. Punctual, good-looking, and brimming with confidence, he seemed like someone I could actually have fun with. But the moment he arrived at my place, he chose to park himself on the tiniest chair in my apartment instead of sitting next to me on the couch. That was red flag number one. Five minutes in, he was snoring like a chainsaw. Nothing says romance like falling asleep mid-date.

And let's not forget about the cute guy who claimed he was twenty-five, in town for the summer, and looking for some casual romance. He was sweet, almost too sweet—innocent, even. I should've known something was off. We went out for drinks, but when we got to the bar, he was denied entry. Turns out my "summer fling" was a nineteen-year-old carny, fresh off the circus circuit.

Seriously, what is wrong with me?

To say that my dating life has been a disaster is putting it lightly—like calling a shipwreck a minor inconvenience. But unlike the spinster I'm determined not to become, I keep throwing myself into the fray, hoping that the next swipe or awkward first date might lead to something real. Yet, here I am again, on the cusp of another evening, not planning to meet Mr. Right but instead heading toward something more reliable: a good book.

Right now, the only thing I can think about is heading to the bookstore, finding tonight's perfect book boyfriend, and curling up in bed with a glass of wine. It's not exactly the kind of passion I'd envisioned for my life, but it's dependable—and there's something comforting in that.

Stepping into Spellbound Stories feels like slipping into a warm bath after a long, cold day. This little corner of the world is my sanctuary. The fantasy décor, with its floating bookshelves and enchanted forest murals, stirs something magical inside me every time. And then there's that unmistakable new book smell that greets you at the door, lingering in every nook and cranny. It's pure bliss.

And, of course, there's Park. The adorable, off-limits clerk who's been the subject of one too many of my fantasies. Unfortunately, those fantasies were dashed when I learned that we're both playing for the same team—team "seeking men." But if nothing else, that revelation has given us a solid foundation for friendship. Plus, he always knows exactly which book will get me through the night, which is a skill I value almost as much as his good looks.

"Welcome!" Lea's voice chimed from behind the counter, carrying that sing-song cheerfulness that made her the perfect fit for a bookstore like this. "How are you doing today, Jessa?"

"Doing as well as can be expected," I replied with a smile. "Just here to find my date for the night."

"Park's putting out a couple of new titles right now," Lea said, nodding toward the back of the store.

"Perfect, thanks!" I followed her gesture, weaving through the aisles until I spotted Park, carefully arranging books on a shelf. "Hey, cutie," I called out.

He glanced over his shoulder, a playful smirk already forming on his lips. "If it isn't my favorite spinster," he teased.

I nudged his shoulder with mine, rolling my eyes. "Spinster or not, I'm on the hunt for love tonight. Think you can hook a girl up?"

He leaned back against the shelf, crossing his arms with a grin. "What's the request?"

"I'm looking for the perfect lover," I said, my voice taking on a dramatic tone. "Tall, confident, maybe a little on the kinky side. Any chance he's hiding out in an obscure corner, just waiting for me to discover him?"

Park raised an eyebrow, his expression turning

thoughtful. "Hmm... well," he began, setting the books down on a nearby table. "Considering your... let's say, eclectic reading tastes..."

I shot him a mock-indignant look. "What exactly is that supposed to mean?"

He laughed, the sound warm and familiar. "Let me clarify—considering your willingness to dive into whatever weird and wonderful book I hand you, I think I have just the thing."

I tried to stifle my grin but failed miserably. "When you put it that way, you know I'm game. Bring it on."

Park didn't say another word. Instead, he led me to a section of the store that seemed almost hidden from the rest—an alcove tucked away. He ran his fingers along the spines, finally pausing at a thick, leather-bound book. He pulled it off the shelf and handed it to me with a flourish.

I took the book. "What do we have here? The Beginner's Guide to Romance Magic," I said hesitantly. "I was thinking something I could read one-handed, if you catch my drift."

Park chuckled. "Oh, I hear you loud and clear, Jessa. Turn to page seventy-eight. I think you might find something interesting there."

I flipped through the book and stopped on The Perfect Lover Spell. "Well, I mean, I did say I was looking for the perfect lover. I just didn't think, you know, magic was the answer."

"Hey, if it doesn't hurt anyone, what's the harm in trying it?" Park suggested.

"Okay, let's say I bite. I buy the book and add," I glanced at the page, "cloves to a potion. What happens? Will the man of my dreams come knocking on my door? Like magic?"

Park shrugged. "I don't know. But what I will say is that I did one of the spells, and then I met Ben. I'm not saying I met him because of the spell, but I'm not saying I didn't either."

"You liar. This book just came out, and you met Ben last Thanksgiving." I crossed my arms.

"Okay, well, that's true. But please?" he pouted.

"I'm not your guinea pig, Park."

"Yes, you are. And I need to know if it works. For research," he said, his eyes growing larger and more puppy-like.

"Fine," I conceded.

"You'll do the spell?" Park asked, far more excited than he should be.

"Yes, but you're giving me your employee discount on this one," I said. "Especially if I have to go to the store to buy ingredients for this experiment."

"Done."

bryce

The sun hung low in the sky, casting a golden glow over the rolling hills that stretched beyond the village of Glenmore. I stood at the edge of my family's farm, leaning against the old wooden fence, watching the cows lazily grazing in the meadow. The air was fresh and crisp, a perfect reflection of the quaint life I led in this corner of Scotland.

"Oi, Bryce!" called a voice from behind me. It was Hamish, my neighbor, ambling down the path with a wide grin on his face. "Daydreaming again, are we?"

I chuckled, turning to face the older man. "Aye, just wondering what it would be like to see the world beyond these hills."

Hamish shook his head, a knowing twinkle in his eye. "Ah, the wanderlust of youth. But ye'll find there's plenty of adventure to be had right here in Glenmore if ye look hard enough."

I smiled, though my thoughts lingered elsewhere. While I loved my village, the longing for something more tugged at my heart. At thirty, I felt the weight of the years that had passed without the adventures I'd dreamed of in my youth. I imagined bustling cities, vibrant cultures, and the thrill of the unknown—all things I could only dream of while tending to the farm.

As we chatted, the faint sound of bagpipes drifted through the air from the village square, where the annual Glenmore Highland Games were underway. The event was a local highlight, a blend of tradition and friendly competition that brought everyone together.

"Are ye comin' to the games later, Bryce?" Hamish asked, his eyes alight with anticipation. "Ye might even find a bonnie lass to keep ye company."

I laughed, though I felt a familiar pang of yearning. "Perhaps, Hamish. But the lass who'll steal my heart might need to have a bit of magic about her," I said with a wink.

With a final wave, Hamish continued on his way, leaving me to my thoughts. As I made my way back to the farmhouse, I couldn't shake the feeling that my life was meant for more than this pastoral existence.

Inside the cozy kitchen, the aroma of freshly baked scones filled the air, and my mother, Moira, bustled about, her hands dusted with flour. "There you are, Bryce. I thought I'd heard you outside."

I kissed her cheek with a grin. "I thought I'd come and steal one of your scones, Mum."

Moira laughed softly, her eyes filled with affection. "You remind me so much of your father at your age. Always dreaming. But remember, sometimes the greatest adventures come when you least expect them."

As I helped set the table for tea, my mind wandered to the stories my father used to tell of our ancestors: fierce Highland warriors who embraced the unknown with courage. It was a legacy I felt in my bones, a reminder that the world was vast and full of possibilities.

Later, as twilight descended upon Glenmore, I walked the familiar path to the village square. The sound of laughter and music grew louder with each step, drawing me into the heart of the celebration. The Highland Games were in full swing, with kilt-clad competitors showcasing their strength and skill.

I joined a group of friends near the caber toss, exchanging jokes and playful banter. Despite the lively atmosphere, my mind wandered elsewhere. I was lost in thought when a sudden gust of wind swept through the square, causing the banners to flutter wildly. I shivered as a strange sensation coursed through me, as if the universe were shifting around me.

The feeling was fleeting, but it left me with an inexplicable sense of anticipation. I shook my head, dismissing it as the excitement of the games. Yet, deep down, I couldn't shake the feeling that something extraordinary was on the horizon.

As the night wore on, I found myself alone on a hill overlooking the village, the stars twinkling like a thousand distant dreams. I sighed, the cool breeze ruffling my hair.

"Maybe tomorrow," I whispered to the night sky. "Maybe tomorrow will be the day everything changes."

jessa

The list of ingredients are as follows:

A cauldron of water – Boil then turn to down to a simmer.

Cinnamon

Ginger Root

Star Anise

Lavender

Cloves

Fresh Rose Peddles

1 Pink Candle

ropping ginger root into the simmering pot, I scanned the list of ingredients again. I double-checked my grocery haul splayed

out on the countertop—everything seemed to be here. I stole another bite of my orange chicken and fried rice before going back to the spell book.

With any love spell, your intentions must be clear, infused with positive energy, and come from an honest heart. What you're asking from the universe must be in harmony with the world you live in. Remember, anything you put into the universe will come back threefold—whether positive or negative.

Be sure to carefully consider what you ask for. There's nothing worse than asking for someone you think you want in your life, only to find out they're quite horrible for you—and worse, difficult to get rid of. Instead, focus on the feelings and qualities you desire in a lover.

Do you want a one-night stand or marriage? Do you need someone who's a caretaker or someone who can take control? What kind of sex life do you desire? What values should your future mate have? Considerations like money, family, kids, and religion are all crucial for a successful love spell.

The Perfect Lover Spell is best performed on a Friday, as Friday is the day of Aphrodite. When you have a clear idea of what you want in a lover, you're ready to perform the spell.

"Light a pink candle," I read aloud, spinning around to grab the candle. The only pink one the grocery store had was a seven-day candle with a picture of Dolly Parton on the outside. "Alright, Dolly, let's do this thing." I struck a match. "Let there be light."

Add the cinnamon, cloves, lavender, ginger root, and star anise, to the cauldron.

I grabbed the last two ingredients on the list, then dropped in the ginger root and the little star anise into the simmering pot. "Okay, Perfect Lover Spell, let's make some magic."

Before you start the incantation, it's best to be naked. Nudity helps break down our walls and allows us to be more open and vulnerable. No barriers between you and the life you desire.

Per the instructions, I stripped off my clothes. If this is some stupid joke, Park will never hear the end of it.

Naked, standing over a pot of bubbling water with

the lit Dolly candle at the ready, I couldn't help but smile.

After you say the first part of the incantation, add one rose petal for every attribute of your perfect lover. Then, say the final incantation.

I assumed my silver pot would do instead of a cauldron. But if this goes awry—again—I'm blaming Park. Plain and simple.

I took a deep breath.

"You must believe for it to work," I said aloud. Wasn't that what Park told me before I left?

I closed my eyes and thought about all the horrible dates and boyfriends I've had. All the shitty lovers who made me doubt my own attractiveness. The boys who toyed with my heart and made me feel less than. I didn't want to bring that kind of nasty energy into this experience. If I'm going to do a love spell, I'm going to give it everything.

I took another deep breath and tried to channel the future I wanted. The book said manifestation is about speaking as if you already have everything you desire.

You're bringing your future to the present. Try saying, "I have the perfect lover," instead of, "I want the perfect lover."

I don't know if I fully understand the larger universal implications, but I can play ball. Okay, I think I'm ready for this.

I took a long pull from my glass of wine. Yeah, I wasn't about to perform magic for the first time sober. I read the incantation to myself one more time.

It's now or never, Jessa.

"Aphrodite, Goddess of love and beauty, bring to me a lover worthy of me, and I worthy of them," I began, taking a breath and grabbing my rose petals. I dropped one into the pot with each desire. "My lover is a kind man. He is a caregiver who understands what it means to care for your partner. My lover makes me laugh. I never worry about how they feel or what we mean to each other; there is complete honesty and trust between us. We complete each other—mind, body, and soul. Intellectually, sexually, and spiritually. There is an understanding between us that transcends this human existence. We fulfill each other sexually. He was made for me, and I for him. Our desire for one another never wavers. He is my perfect lover, partner, and soulmate," I said, feeling my words resonate through every fiber of my being.

"Oh, and he has a birthmark on his ass," I added, just to ensure I'd know if the spell worked. Letting my last petal fall into the water, I felt something inside me begin to grow.

I glanced at the book again for the closing words. "Goddess Aphrodite, I submit myself to you. Bring my perfect lover to me. So mote it be, three by three by three."

bryce

The wood shop was my sanctuary, filled with the scent of freshly cut lumber. I spent countless hours here, surrounded by the comforting aroma of sawdust and the rhythmic sounds of tools shaping wood. On any given day, you could find me crafting furniture, restoring antiques, or simply tinkering with ideas that danced around in my mind. The family business wasn't bustling by any means, but it was familiar, and it was mine. Today, however, was different.

I was sanding down a rough edge on an old chair when a sudden gust of wind whipped through the open window. The weather in Scotland was as fickle as a cat, but this breeze felt peculiar. It carried an energy, a strange tingling that seemed to hum through the air and settle in me, penetrating my skin, worming its way down into my bones.

Brushing it off as nothing more than an odd draft, I refocused on my work. But the feeling didn't leave. It intensified, becoming almost electric, like the air before a storm. I set the sandpaper down—something prickled at the back of my neck.

Before I could ponder further, the world around me twisted and blurred. My workshop dissolved into a whirlwind of colors and light. My heart pounded, threatening to break free from my chest. Panic rose as I grasped at the bench, trying to anchor myself in reality.

"What the bloody—" I began, but the words were snatched away as the vortex swallowed me whole.

The sensation was dizzying, like being caught in a maelstrom, tumbling through space and time. My stomach lurched, and my mind raced with a thousand questions. What was happening? Was this some sort of dream? Had I inhaled too many varnish fumes?

Then, just as suddenly as it began, the storm ceased. I landed with a thud on a soft carpet, blinking against the sudden brightness.

Disoriented, I took in my surroundings. I was no longer in my workshop, that was for sure. Instead, I found myself in a cozy living room filled with the scent of lavender and vanilla. Books lined the walls, and a simmering pot bubbled nearby, emitting fragrant steam.

I blinked again, struggling to make sense of the impossible. It was like stepping into a scene from one of the old stories my father used to tell about Highlanders lost to time and another world.

"W-where am I?" I muttered to myself, still trying to catch my breath.

From the corner of my eye, there was movement. A woman, wide-eyed and clearly as startled as I was, stood just a few feet away. Her hair cascaded in wild curls, and her skin was flushed from what I assumed was a combination of shock and embarrassment.

And then it hit me: this goddess was stark naked.

My brain short-circuited for a moment, and all I could do was stare, my mouth opening and closing like a daft fish. The woman let out a startled yelp, snatching a nearby blanket and wrapping it around herself with a speed that would have impressed an Olympic athlete.

"Who are you?" she demanded, eyes narrowing suspiciously. "And what are you doing in my apartment?"

I tried to find my voice, but it seemed to have taken a temporary leave of absence. "I—uh—well, I was just in my workshop, and then there was this—this whirlwind, and now I'm here." My words tumbled out in a thick Scottish brogue, no doubt sounding as bewildered as I felt.

Her expression shifted from suspicion to confusion, her grip on the blanket loosening slightly. "A whirlwind? What, like you caught a tornado here, Dorothy?"

I shook my head. "I don't know who Dorothy is. It was like a magical teleportation spell or something." I put my hands up. "I've never been the subject of magic or tornado-induced transportation before. It's all new to me."

Her eyes narrowed.

I shrugged helplessly. "One moment I was in Scotland, and the next, I'm in your living room."

"Scotland?" she echoed, eyebrows shooting up. "You're saying you're from Scotland?"

I nodded, trying to make sense of the situation while attempting to ignore the surge of awareness that came with her standing so close. "Aye. Name's Bryce MacGregor," I said, my voice a bit huskier than I intended. "And you are?"

"Jessa," she replied, her gaze softening slightly. "Jessa Owens."

We stood there, both of us grappling with the absurdity of the situation. It felt like a scene straight out of a romance novel, where destiny—or perhaps a touch of magic—intervened in the most unexpected ways. The air between us seemed to hum with unspoken possibilities, leaving me wondering if fate was playing a cruel joke or if there was something more at play.

"Okay, let's just take a breath," Jessa said, her voice betraying her effort to regain composure. "There's got to be some logical explanation for this."

I chuckled. "Logical explanation? Lass, I've just

been whisked across the globe and landed in a room with a naked woman. Logic seems to have taken a holiday."

To my surprise, she laughed—a bright, genuine sound that cut through the tension, making the situation feel a little less surreal. "Fair point. This is... unusual, to say the least."

I couldn't help but grin. Jessa was undeniably charming, her wild curls framing a face that managed to look both fierce and soft at the same time. Even in this bizarre scenario, I found myself drawn to her—a pull that was more than just the situation. It was in the way she carried herself, a blend of confidence and vulnerability that stirred something deep within me. I realized, with a jolt, that I didn't want to look away.

"Where is here?" I asked, scanning the room for any context clues that might ground me in reality.

"You're in Coral Cove. The Pacific Northwest of the United States," she replied.

"Really?" I asked, eyebrows raising in surprise.

Jessa nodded, a hint of amusement in her eyes.

"Weird," I murmured, still processing the strangeness of it all, yet unable to shake the feeling that there was something extraordinary about this moment—and about her.

"So, Bryce," she said, her voice softening as her eyes met mine, a curious blend of amusement and something else flickering in their depths. "Do you have any idea how we're going to get you back to Scotland?"

The way she said my name, like a secret only the two of us shared, sent a shiver down my spine.

I shrugged, glancing around the room as if the answer might be hiding in a corner. "I've no clue. But maybe there's a reason I ended up here."

Jessa eyed me thoughtfully, the corners of her lips twitching in a half-smile. "A reason, huh? Like destiny or magic?"

I tilted my head, weighing the possibility. "Perhaps. Or maybe the universe just has a peculiar sense of humor."

We both laughed, a shared moment of camaraderie amidst the chaos. Neither of us had the answers, but there was something oddly comforting about facing the unknown together.

"Well, until we figure it out," Jessa said, her voice dropping to a low, almost conspiratorial tone as she gestured toward the couch, "make yourself at home. I'm going to find some clothes." She turned to leave, but not before our eyes locked for a heartbeat longer than necessary, the air between us charged with a tension neither of us dared to acknowledge. Yet.

"Don't do it for me," I teased, winking as I settled into the plush cushions, marveling at the strange twist of fate that had brought me here. An adventure indeed, I thought, as I watched Jessa move around the room with an air of determination.

In that moment, as I sat in her living room, the reality of my situation began to sink in. But instead of fear or confusion, what I felt was a pulse of pure, unfiltered excitement. My eyes followed Jessa as she moved around the room, my mind spinning with possibilities. Maybe, just maybe, this was the adventure I'd been waiting for all along—and perhaps, if the universe had its way, it wasn't just an adventure of place, but of the heart as well.

jessa

The silence in the room was almost comical. If someone had told me this morning that I'd be standing in my living room, wrapped in a blanket, talking to a Scotsman who looked like he'd stepped out of a Highlander romance, I would've laughed in their face. Yet, here we were, both of us equally perplexed and trying to make sense of it all.

"What's the date?" Bryce asked, his brow furrowing slightly as he scanned the room like a time traveler trying to place his coordinates.

I shook my head, trying to keep the absurdity from overwhelming me. "You look pretty present-day to me," I replied, my voice barely masking the rising hysteria.

"Is it twenty-fourteen?" he asked again, his tone insistent, eyes locking onto mine with a seriousness that sent a shiver down my spine.

I blinked, my brain doing somersaults. "Are you serious?"

"I mean, I think life is more enjoyable with a laugh, but on this point, I'm wholly serious," he replied, his thick Scottish brogue making even the most ridiculous statements sound like sweet promises.

I watched him settle onto my couch as if he belonged there, a bemused grin tugging at his lips. He looked far too comfortable for someone who'd just been plucked from his cozy workshop in Scotland and dropped into my living room like a very sexy, very confusing gift from the universe. The whole situation felt like a fever dream, and I half-expected to wake up any moment.

But Bryce... well, he didn't seem like he was in any rush to leave. In fact, he looked almost amused by the whole ordeal, like this was just another quirky adventure life had thrown his way. Maybe it was the rugged charm, or the way his eyes sparkled with mischief despite the craziness, but I found myself relaxing, if only a little.

"I suppose putting you on a plane is out of the question. You're about ten years behind," I said, attempting to inject some humor into the madness.

"Ten years?" Bryce echoed, his brows knitting together in surprise. "Was it a good ten years?"

I cringed, not sure how to sugarcoat the past decade.

He waved a hand dismissively, his tone light despite

the bizarre situation. "Don't tell me. I'd rather find out for myself."

I turned away, beginning to pace the room, clutching the blanket around me like it was a lifeline. Magic wasn't real. Or, at least, that's what I kept telling myself, even as the evidence sat there, looking every bit the part of a displaced Scotsman.

"Okay, Jessa," I muttered to myself, trying to regain control of my racing thoughts. "Let's break this down. Somehow, you performed a spell and conjured up a man. Not just any man, but a man from Scotland, and apparently, from ten years in the past. What are the odds?" I paused, wondering if my friend Park had spiked my drink with something hallucinogenic. This couldn't be real.

"Ye look like you're trying to solve a grand mystery, lass," Bryce observed, his voice teasing yet warm, like a gentle nudge out of my spiraling thoughts.

I stopped pacing and faced him, trying not to be distracted by how ridiculously handsome he was. "I just don't understand how any of this is possible. I mean, I did a spell as a joke," I admitted, throwing my hands up in exasperation. "Magic isn't real. People don't just appear out of thin air."

"If magic isn't real, why were you practicing it?" Bryce asked, his tone curious yet pointed, like he was genuinely trying to understand the logic—or lack thereof.

That pulled me up short. "I... well, maybe a tiny

part of me wanted to believe in something more," I confessed, suddenly feeling very exposed under his gaze.

"So maybe people do appear out of thin air after all?" Bryce smirked, leaning back on the couch as if he'd just won an argument. "I'm living proof of it, am I not?"

I wanted to argue, to cling to some semblance of reality, but the evidence was sitting right there, all six feet of him, rugged and undeniably real. "This can't be happening," I muttered, more to myself than to him.

Bryce leaned forward, resting his elbows on his knees, his eyes gleaming with a mix of amusement and seriousness. "Ye're not the only one feeling out of sorts. I was just a simple man, working on a chair, and now I'm here, talking to you. And if magic's the culprit, then we'll just have to figure out how to make it work in reverse, aye?"

I sighed, the weight of the situation finally sinking in. "Yeah, about that... Even if we figure out how to reverse the spell, you're kind of stuck around here for the moment."

His brow furrowed deeply, a hint of vulnerability seeping through his confident demeanor. "What do you mean?"

I hesitated, trying to find the right words. "Well, you said you're from Scotland, right? From ten years ago?"

He nodded, the confusion evident on his face.

"Even if we could get you a plane ticket, you don't have any ID, and it's not just that," I continued, watching as the realization began to dawn on him. "You're technically not even in the right year. If you go back, your friends and family will think you've been missing for the last decade. You can't just pop back into their lives like nothing happened."

The realization hit him, and his expression shifted from bemusement to concern. "Ten years? That's... quite a long time to be gone. My family would think I disappeared, or worse."

"Exactly," I said, the gravity of the situation settling heavily between us. "We need to figure out how this happened and, more importantly, how to reverse it. Until then, you're stuck here."

Bryce leaned back, rubbing his chin thoughtfully, a slow grin spreading across his face. "Stuck in the future with a beautiful woman. There are worse fates, I suppose," he quipped, though the smile didn't quite reach his eyes.

I couldn't help but chuckle, despite the storm of emotions swirling around us. "Don't get any ideas, MacGregor. This isn't some romance novel where we fall in love at first sight."

He raised an eyebrow, his playful demeanor returning. "Who said anything about love? I'm just trying to make the best of a strange situation."

I crossed my arms, the blanket slipping slightly, reminding me of my less-than-ideal wardrobe situation. "Good. As long as we're clear on that. No magic spell is going to make me fall for a man I accidentally conjured."

Bryce nodded, but I could see the hint of challenge in his eyes. "Understood, lass. But I'm still curious about this magic of yours. How exactly did you manage to bring me here?"

I sighed, realizing it was time to come clean. My cheeks warmed under his gaze. "I was just messing around with a book that a friend recommended. It was called *The Beginner's Guide to Romance Magic.* There was this spell—The Perfect Lover Spell—and, well, I guess it worked a little too well."

His eyes lit up with interest, a mischievous glint appearing. "And what exactly were ye hopin' to conjure with this spell?"

I felt the blush deepen. "Not a real person, that's for sure. Just, you know, the idea of the perfect partner. Someone who's kind, funny, and maybe a little bit magical."

Bryce chuckled, the sound warm and rich, sending a shiver down my spine. "And here I am. Though I'm not sure how magical I am, beyond the whole time-travelin' Scotsman thing."

Heat bloomed in my center. "Yeah, well, you've got a lot to live up to, MacGregor," I teased, feeling the tension between us ease slightly.

We shared a moment of silence, both of us lost in thought about the bizarre twist our lives had taken.

Despite my initial disbelief, I couldn't deny the connection forming between us. It was as if the universe had thrown us together for a reason, even if I wasn't ready to admit it.

"So, what's our plan, then?" Bryce asked, breaking the silence with that same playful tone. "How do we unravel this mystery?"

I considered the question, feeling the weight of our predicament settle in. "First, we need to do some research. I'll check the book and see if there are any clues about reversing the spell. Maybe we can find answers online, too."

Bryce nodded, determination in his eyes. "And until then, I suppose we're partners in this strange adventure?" He reached out his hand.

"Yeah, partners," I agreed, slipping my hand into his. My heart fluttered at the contact.

"The perfect lover, aye?" he said, gently rubbing the back of my hand, his voice dropping to a low, teasing rumble.

I nodded, unable to tear my gaze away from his. His touch sent a jolt of electricity through me, making my heart skip a beat. There was a softness in his eyes, a mischievous glint that made me both nervous and excited. I couldn't deny it any longer—Bryce was gorgeous. His dark red hair was tousled in a way that suggested he was born to star in a Highland fantasy, and his piercing blue eyes seemed to see right through me, right into my soul.

Bryce didn't let go of my hand. Instead, he gently pulled me down onto the couch beside him. The world seemed to tilt on its axis as I sank into the cushions, feeling the heat radiating from his body.

"I've got to say, you did quite a job with that spell, lass," he teased, his voice a delicious rumble that made my skin tingle. "If you were aiming for the perfect lover, I'm afraid I might disappoint. But I'll do my best to rise to the occasion."

"Is that right?" I challenged, feeling bolder than I had in years. "Well, I'm a pretty demanding woman, you know. You might have your work cut out for you."

His grin widened, full of confidence and that irresistible charm. "Aye, but I'm a quick study."

Without another word, he leaned in and kissed me, his lips soft and tentative against mine. The world fell away, leaving just the two of us in that moment, suspended in time. It was like fireworks behind my eyes —dazzling, electric, and utterly breathtaking.

I melted into him, my mind a whirl of emotions as the kiss deepened. My thoughts flickered back to the spell, how I conjured him out of thin air with nothing but words and wishes. Yet in that moment, he felt as real and solid as anything I'd ever known.

Bryce's hands moved to my waist, pulling me closer until I was practically in his lap. The blanket slipped, exposing more of my skin to the cool air. I gasped against his mouth, and he chuckled, a low, sexy sound that made my pulse race.

"Ye're more beautiful than I could have imagined," he murmured, his fingers tracing delicate lines along my bare shoulders, leaving a trail of fire in their wake.

I shivered, both from his touch and his words. "You imagined me?"

He pulled back slightly, his eyes twinkling with mischief. "Of course. A woman who could conjure me from ten years in the past and halfway around the world had to be something extraordinary."

I laughed, feeling the tension melt away, replaced by a delicious heat that spread through my entire body. "Well, I did say I wanted someone a little magical."

"And here I am," he replied, shifting beneath me so that I straddled him, the blanket slipping further down my body.

His hands moved with a gentle but insistent purpose, sliding the blanket away to reveal my breasts. His gaze traveled over me, reverent and appreciative, and I felt a flush of heat that had nothing to do with embarrassment.

"You're incredible, Jessa," he said, his voice hushed with awe. "I don't think I've ever seen anyone so stunning."

A smile tugged at my lips, but words seemed to fail me. Instead, I reached up, threading my fingers through his hair, loving the feel of his dark red locks against my skin.

With each kiss that Bryce trailed along my collarbone, my skin erupted in a symphony of goosebumps, amplifying the sensation of his touch. His hands followed the path his mouth set, exploring with a touch that was both teasing and tender.

"I suppose I'm just about the luckiest man alive to have been conjured by someone as remarkable as you," he murmured against my skin, his lips curving into a playful smile.

"Don't get too cocky, MacGregor," I warned, though my voice was breathless, and my heart was pounding in my chest.

"Ah, but ye like me cocky," he playfully teased, leaving a trail of gentle kisses along my shoulder, his hands caressing every inch of exposed skin. Every place he touched me left fire in its wake.

I sucked in a breath as his touch moved lower, tracing lines down my body and removing the blanket entirely. It was all I could do to hold onto him, to keep from losing myself completely in the sensations he stirred.

"Words," I whispered, my voice a mere breath of sound. "I need words."

Bryce chuckled, lifting me effortlessly in his arms. "Words are overrated, love. Actions speak louder, don't ye think?"

He carried me toward the bedroom, every step sending anticipation humming through me. I couldn't help but giggle, feeling like a teenager sneaking away for a forbidden tryst.

"This way?" he asked, nudging the door open with his foot, his grin wide and irresistible.

I nodded, unable to find my voice, pointing him toward the bed that awaited us.

He laid me down gently, straddling over me with a grace that belied his strength. "Ye know, your room is as enchanting as you are," he said, casting a glance around the eclectic décor that filled the space. "I half expected unicorns and fairy dust."

I laughed, feeling warmth blossom in my chest. "Sorry to disappoint. Just me and a lot of books."

"Well, that's a sight I'll never tire of," he replied, his fingers tracing a line along my jaw before capturing my lips in another searing kiss.

It was everything I'd imagined and more—the perfect blend of passion and playfulness that left me breathless. I tugged at his shirt, eager to feel more of him, to discover every inch of the man I'd somehow conjured.

"Too many clothes," I murmured against his lips, my hands deftly working to free him from the fabric that separated us.

He obliged with a smirk, tossing his shirt aside to reveal a physique that was lean and muscular. I drank him in, my eyes wide with appreciation as I traced the lines of his muscles with eager fingers.

"Ye approve, then?" he asked, his voice a low rumble that sent heat pooling in my belly.

"Very much," I breathed, feeling the connection between us deepen with every touch, every kiss.

His hands explored my body with a reverence that sucked all the air out of my lungs. All words died on my lips. Soon we were tangled together, a symphony of limbs and laughter and teasing caresses.

I found myself above him once more, straddling his hips as he gazed up at me with an intensity that made my heart skip a beat. He was beautiful, all tousled hair and smoldering eyes. The mere thought of him being here, with me, in this moment sent a thrill coursing through my veins.

As his hard cock entered me, a moan escaped my lips. The world fell away, leaving only us, wrapped in a magical cocoon of warmth and desire. We stayed like that for a long moment, my body adjusting to the girth of him. I moved above him, each slow thrust igniting a firestorm of pleasure that built with intensity.

Bryce's hands found my hips again, guiding me with a firm touch, his thumbs tracing patterns across my skin that sent delicious shivers racing through me.

His touch drifted lower, finding my clit, the sensitive bundle of nerves that sent shockwaves of pleasure coursing through my veins. My breath hitched, my insides coiling in on themselves. With one touch, I was lost to the sensation, to the overwhelming bliss that surged through me in waves.

When release finally claimed me, it was with a force

that shattered every thought, every worry, leaving only the blinding euphoria of the moment.

I cried out, my body trembling with the after-shocks of the most explosive orgasm I'd ever experienced.

As I collapsed against him, breathless and spent, Bryce wrapped his arms around me, holding me close. The world slowly came back into focus, and I found myself nestled against him, feeling a sense of peace and contentment that was wholly unexpected.

"Ye're quite the enchantress, Jessa," he said, pressing a soft kiss to my temple. "I've a feeling this adventure is just beginning."

I smiled, unable to deny the truth of his words. Maybe magic was real after all. And maybe, just maybe, I'd found my perfect lover in the most unexpected of ways.

bryce

The morning light filtered softly through the curtains, casting a warm, golden glow over the room. I lay still, listening to the rhythmic sound of Jessa's breathing beside me, her chest rising and falling in a slow, peaceful rhythm. My mind, however, was anything but peaceful—a whirlwind of thoughts raced through it, trying to make sense of the past few hours.

This morning, I'd been nothing more than a man sanding down a chair in Scotland. Now, I was lying in bed with a woman who had somehow conjured me out of my life and into the future. It was surreal, impossible even, but there was something about it that felt... right. And that scared the hell out of me. The longer I lay there, the more doubts crept in.

Sure, Jessa was enchanting—wild hair, expressive eyes, a laugh that could light up the darkest room. She was the kind of woman who turned heads, made you forget your own name. But the idea that I could fall in love with her? That seemed far-fetched. I couldn't stay with someone who'd summoned me with magic. I had a life back in Scotland—one I needed to return to, for better or worse.

Careful not to wake her, I slipped out of bed and quietly pulled on my clothes before wandering into the living room. The remnants of our night together were scattered around, but my thoughts were elsewhere. I had to figure out how to reverse this spell, how to get back to my time.

Despite the undeniable chemistry between us, this was temporary. A fluke of magic that needed fixing. I wasn't meant to be here, in this time, with this woman. As I paced the room, though, part of me couldn't help but be drawn to her—like maybe there was a reason for all of this, something more at play than just magic.

A soft rustle of sheets signaled that Jessa was waking up. I turned to see her standing in the doorway, wrapped in a blanket, her eyes sleepy but curious as she looked at me.

"Good morning," she said, her voice heavy with sleep. "You're up early."

"Aye," I replied, trying to keep my tone light. "Too many thoughts running through my head."

She joined me on the couch, tucking her legs beneath her and pulling the blanket tighter around her shoulders. "I get it. It's a lot to take in."

We sat in comfortable silence for a moment, the events of the night still hanging between us like a charged wire. I knew we had to talk, figure out what had happened and, more importantly, how to fix it.

"So," I began, turning to face her. "This spell of yours—the one that brought me here—any idea how to reverse it?"

She sighed, running a hand through her tousled hair. "I was hoping you had some brilliant insight. I've never done anything like this before."

"Well, we've got to start somewhere," I said, trying to be practical even as my mind raced with a thousand questions. "Maybe that book you mentioned? It might have some answers."

Jessa nodded, her eyes meeting mine with a spark of determination. "I'll grab it. There might be something we missed."

She retrieved the book from the table, flipping through its pages with a focused intensity that made her even more attractive. There was something about the way she tackled problems head-on that I found irresistible—her strength, her resolve, the way she didn't back down.

We spent the morning poring over the book, jotting down notes, tossing around ideas on how to reverse the spell. It was like working on a complex puzzle, each piece needing to fit perfectly for us to see the full picture. And as strange as it was, I found myself enjoying it—the challenge, the way our minds seemed to sync in this strange dance of problem-solving.

"Here," Jessa said, pointing to a passage in the book. "This part talks about reversing spells. Maybe we can use some of these principles to send you back."

I leaned in closer, reading over her shoulder. Her scent—fresh and floral with a hint of spice—filled my senses. "Aye, it's worth a shot. If we can gather the right ingredients, maybe we can make this work."

As we discussed our plan, the connection between us seemed to grow stronger, as if the universe was weaving our fates together for a reason. Despite my initial resistance, I couldn't deny the attraction, the bond that was forming. It felt as real as anything I'd ever known.

After what felt like hours of intense focus, my stomach rumbled loudly enough to make us both pause. I looked at Jessa, and she smiled, a playful glint in her eyes.

"Sounds like someone's ready for a break," she teased.

I chuckled, rubbing the back of my neck. "Aye, it seems spellcasting is hungry work."

Jessa stretched, closing the book with a soft thud. "Why don't we take a break? I could use a bite to eat too."

I glanced at her, feeling a tug of familiarity despite the strangeness of our situation. "I'd be happy to make us something, though I cannae promise much beyond a simple meal."

"Be my guest," she said with a wave toward the kitchen. "Just don't be surprised if you find more condiments than actual food in there."

Curious, I opened the fridge, only to find it nearly barren—some takeout containers, a half-empty carton of milk, and a lone stick of butter. I raised an eyebrow, turning back to her with a wry grin.

"Looks like I'd need a bit of magic to make a meal out of this," I quipped.

Jessa laughed, the sound bright and infectious. "Guilty as charged. How about we head out for lunch instead? There's this little place—Golden Chopsticks. Nothing fancy, but they make the best orange chicken."

The idea of stepping out into this unfamiliar world felt daunting, but something about her smile put me at ease. "That sounds perfect," I agreed. "Though if we're going out, I might need to clean up a bit."

Jessa's eyes sparkled with a teasing glint. "I was just thinking the same thing. I need a shower, and you, my dear Scotsman, are more than welcome to join."

A thrill shot through me at her invitation, and I found myself grinning. "When in Rome, aye?"

She led me to the bathroom, revealing a space that was nothing short of a modern marvel. The shower was immense, the kind you'd find in a luxury spa, with no doors or curtains—just sleek tiles and an open design with three showerheads arranged to hit you from every angle.

"This is... impressive," I admitted, taking it all in. "Dare I say, intimidating."

Jessa chuckled, stepping into the shower with a grace that was downright mesmerizing. "It's why I chose this place. The shower made it worth it."

I followed her, the warmth of the water cascading over us as the showerheads sprang to life, enveloping us in a steamy, sensual embrace. The sensation was divine, washing away the remnants of doubt and worry that had been gnawing at me since I'd arrived here.

Jessa turned to face me, her gaze locking onto mine as the water traced rivulets down her skin. I was captivated, unable to tear my eyes away from the woman who had somehow brought me into her world. Her hair clung to her shoulders, droplets glistening on her skin like diamonds.

"You're beautiful," I murmured, stepping closer until our bodies were almost touching.

She smiled, reaching for the soap and lathering it in her hands before gently applying it to my chest. Her touch was tender yet electrifying, exploring every contour and muscle with a care that made my pulse quicken and my knees weak.

"You have a birthmark on your bottom," she said.

"Me whole life," I say as she traced fingers on it.

As she worked my body, I took the soap from her, returning the favor by running my hands over her back, her shoulders, and down the curve of her spine. The intimacy of it all was intoxicating, the heat of the shower matching the warmth that blossomed between us.

"Feels nice," she sighed, leaning into me.

I began washing her hair, my fingers massaging her scalp as the fragrant suds enveloped us. It was a simple gesture, but it felt incredibly intimate—like we were sharing something far deeper than just a shower.

As the soap and water rinsed away, Jessa wrapped her arms around me, pressing her body against mine. I held her close, inhaling her scent—fresh, floral, and utterly irresistible.

"Ye smell amazing," I whispered, my lips grazing her ear.

She shivered, and I felt her pulse quicken against my chest. "You're not so bad yourself," she replied, her voice playful but laced with desire.

I couldn't resist any longer. My hands traveled lower, finding her center and coaxing soft moans from her lips. She leaned into me as I explored her with deliberate, gentle strokes, each one drawing her closer to the edge. Her gasps and trembles spurred me on, the fire between us burning hotter with every touch.

Jessa arched against me, her breaths coming in ragged gasps as I continued to pleasure her, my fingers dancing over her sensitive skin. The world narrowed to this moment, this connection, as the water cascaded around us.

Her release was exquisite, a symphony of cries and whispered curses as she reached her peak. I held her through it all, savoring the way she clung to me, the way her body responded to my every touch.

When the aftershocks of her climax finally subsided, Jessa looked up at me with eyes that sparkled with satisfaction and something deeper, something that made my heart skip a beat. "That was... wow," she breathed, still catching her breath.

I grinned, a swell of pride warming me from the inside out. "Glad to be of service, lass."

She kissed me then, a deep, lingering kiss that spoke volumes—more than words ever could. It was a kiss that promised so much more than just physical connection; it was a merging of our worlds, our lives, in a way that felt undeniably right, despite the madness that had brought us together.

As the heat of the moment cooled, Jessa lowered herself to her knees, her intentions clear in the sultry gaze she gave me. My heart raced as I watched her, anticipation building in every fiber of my being.

"Now it's my turn," she purred, her voice dripping with seduction.

Her hands moved with a confident grace, exploring every inch of me as she took me into her mouth, her touch igniting a blaze along my skin. The world around us faded away, leaving only the two of us, the water, and the pure ecstasy that unfurled in a tidal wave between us.

I was lost to it, to her, as her mouth moved over me with a skill that left me gasping, my control slipping with every moment. The tightening in my core grew, an intense, burning pleasure that built with every stroke, every flick of her tongue up and down my thrumming erection.

And when the release finally came, it was like nothing I'd ever experienced—a torrent of pure bliss that left me shaking, my mind adrift on a sea of satisfaction. I couldn't hold back the moan that escaped my lips as I let go, my hands tangling in her wet hair, anchoring me to the moment.

We stayed like that for a while, her holding me through the aftershocks, our breaths mingling in the steam-filled air. When the last of my strength left me, I pulled her up to her feet and into my arms, holding her close as the water continued to rain down on us, a soothing lullaby.

It felt like a dream—this beautiful, impossible escape from reality that I wished could last forever. But as we stood there, wrapped in each other's arms, I realized that maybe, just maybe, this was real. That this connection between us was something more than just the result of a spell gone wrong.

As the water finally began to cool, I pressed a kiss to the top of her head. "We should probably get out before we turn into prunes," I teased, my voice light, but my heart heavy with the weight of what lay ahead.

Jessa chuckled softly, the sound vibrating through

me in the most delicious way. "Yeah, probably a good idea," she agreed, though neither of us made a move to separate just yet.

Eventually, with a reluctant sigh, we turned off the water and stepped out of the shower, drying off with the towels she handed me. The easy banter from before returned, filling the space between us as we dressed.

But there was something different now—an unspoken understanding that this was more than just a fling, more than just a result of magical interference. There was a connection between us that defied logic, defied time itself, and as we got ready to step out into the world, I knew that no matter what happened next, I wasn't ready to let her go.

"Ready for that orange chicken?" she asked, a playful smile tugging at the corners of her lips as she slipped on her shoes.

I nodded, returning her smile with one of my own. "Aye."

jessa

The day was sunny, and the warmth on my skin felt like a gentle reminder that my world had shifted in ways I never could have imagined. As Bryce and I strolled side by side toward Golden Chopsticks, the events of the last twenty-four hours played like a reel in my mind—a surreal mix of magic, disbelief, and an undeniable attraction that had me questioning everything.

Bryce glanced around with wide eyes, his gaze darting from the cars to the people bustling along the sidewalks. He looked like a tourist in a strange new world, and I found it utterly endearing.

"So this is the future," he mused, shaking his head slightly, a mix of awe and confusion in his expression. "Hardly seems real."

"Trust me," I said with a chuckle, nudging him playfully with my elbow. "It feels the same to me. But I have to admit, having a time-traveling Scotsman by my side does add a certain charm to it."

He laughed, a rich, genuine sound that sent a pleasant warmth through my chest. Despite everything, his presence was comforting, like I'd known him forever—even if forever had only been a day.

When we arrived at Golden Chopsticks, the mouthwatering scent of soy sauce and sesame oil clung to the air. The small restaurant was bustling with lunchtime patrons, but we managed to snag a cozy booth by the window.

"This place is delightful," Bryce said, his eyes taking in the lively atmosphere. "Reminds me of the pub back home—always full of life and chatter."

I settled into the booth, grabbing a menu and sliding one across the table to him. "You should try the orange chicken," I suggested, winking at him. "It's like a party in your mouth. Trust me."

He scanned the menu with interest, looking adorably out of place yet somehow perfectly at home in my world. I found myself studying him—how his strong hands held the menu, the way his eyes lit up when he found something intriguing. He was fascinating, and I wanted to know everything about him.

"So," I said, eager to learn more about the man who had quite literally tumbled into my life. "Tell me about Scotland. What's it like?"

Bryce's face lit up, his eyes shining with warmth. "Ah, Scotland. It's beautiful—rolling hills, sweeping moors, the kind of landscape that makes you feel small in the best way possible. You can lose yourself in the mist and feel like you're the only person on earth." He took a sip of water, his gaze far away as he reminisced. "When I left, it was the time of the Highland Games. The air was filled with the sound of bagpipes and the laughter of people gathering for the festivities."

I could almost picture it in my mind, imagining the vibrant colors and lively atmosphere he described. "It sounds magical," I said softly, my voice tinged with longing.

He nodded, his expression thoughtful. "Aye, it is. I run my family's furniture shop there, restoring antiques. There's something about bringing an old piece of wood back to life that just feels... right."

"That sounds fulfilling," I said, genuinely intrigued. "I imagine you must be pretty good with your hands."

Bryce smirked, his eyes sparkling with mischief. "Oh, lass, you've no idea."

I blushed, thinking about the shower—I had some idea. Thankfully, the waiter arrived to take our order, saving me from further embarrassment. As we waited for our food, the conversation flowed naturally, a comfortable rhythm settling between us.

I told him about my job as a high school English teacher, how I loved introducing my students to the world of literature and the power of words.

"You're shaping the future," he said, admiration clear in his tone. "That's no small feat."

I shrugged, feeling a bit shy under his praise. "I try my best. Though, shouldn't you be in a classroom right now, shaping those young minds?"

I laughed, shaking my head. "Today's Saturday, Bryce. You really have lost track of time, haven't you?"

He chuckled, running a hand through his hair, a sheepish grin on his face. "Aye, I suppose I have. This whole time-travel business has me feeling a bit out of sorts."

When our food arrived, Bryce's eyes widened in delight as he tasted the orange chicken. "This is incredible! They don't make anything quite like this back home."

We ate in comfortable silence for a moment, the satisfaction of a good meal adding to the pleasantness of the day. But curiosity got the better of him, and soon he was looking at me with those inquisitive eyes of his.

"So, what's happened in the last ten years? Anything I should be aware of?"

I paused, searching for the right words to distill the last decade into something manageable. "Well, let's see... technology's pretty much taken over every aspect of life. Robots are everywhere, and if you're not careful, they'll be taking your job next. Social media isn't just on your phone anymore—it's in your glasses, your watches, even your TV. Politics? Well, that's been one hell of a roller-coaster. Honestly, I'm not sure you're ready for that ride. And, oh yeah, we survived a global pandemic—not that we've fully figured out what that means yet."

Bryce's eyes widened, clearly startled by the mention of a pandemic. "A pandemic?"

I nodded, giving him a reassuring smile. "Yeah, it was intense. Lockdowns, masks, the whole nine yards. If you're thinking about where to put your money these days," I added, letting a smirk slip through, "ByteDance a solid bet."

Bryce chuckled, the sound tinged with a mix of disbelief and amusement. "That's a lot to process. Maybe being stuck here a while longer isn't such a bad thing. Gives me time to get up to speed."

As we finished our meal, a sense of contentment settled over me. Bryce's company was easy, enjoyable, and it was hard to believe we'd only just met. But the reality of our situation loomed over us, and I knew we needed answers.

"Ready to hit the bookstore?" I asked, hoping we might find some clues about how to reverse the spell. After all, that's where I'd bought the book in the first place.

Bryce nodded, his expression turning serious. "Aye, let's see if we can make sense of this mess."

We left the restaurant and made our way to Spellbound Stories, the bell above the door chiming as we entered. I spotted Park organizing a display near the back.

"Jessa!" he exclaimed, his eyes lighting up when he saw me. But when his gaze shifted to Bryce, his jaw dropped. "Wait a minute... Is this...?"

"Park, meet Bryce MacGregor, straight from 2014," I said, introducing them with a flourish.

Park's eyes widened as he approached, studying Bryce with a mix of awe and disbelief. "I can't believe it. You're really from the past?"

Bryce nodded, extending a hand with that charming smile of his. "That I am. Pleasure to meet ye."

Park shook his hand, still looking incredulous. "I don't know whether to be amazed or terrified."

"We're hoping you can help us figure out how to reverse the spell," I said, cutting to the chase.

Park hesitated, scratching his head. "Well, I got the book from The Arcane Room. Ms. Vesper recommended it. She's kind of an expert in these things."

"Ms. Vesper?" Bryce echoed, glancing at me with curiosity.

"She's kind of a local legend," I explained. "If anyone knows about reversing spells, it'll be her."

Park nodded, a sheepish smile on his face. "I might have mentioned you to her, Jessa. I'm a bit of a romantic meddler, and I thought you deserved more. I had no idea this would happen."

His admission warmed my heart, and I pulled him into a hug. "Thank you, Park. It means a lot."

Bryce chuckled, watching the exchange with amusement. "Looks like I've got ye to thank for bringing a bit of magic into my life."

We left Spellbound Stories with a renewed sense of hope. With Park's information, we had a lead—a chance to unravel the mystery of the spell and perhaps find a way to send Bryce home.

But as we made our way to The Arcane Room, a pang of uncertainty settled in my chest. We were getting closer to finding a solution, but that also meant we were getting closer to saying goodbye. I pushed the thought down, determined to focus on the task at hand.

The Arcane Room was nestled on a quiet street, its exterior as mysterious and enchanting as its name suggested. As we approached, I felt a tingle of anticipation, a mix of excitement and nerves swirling in my stomach.

We entered, and the air was thick with the scent of incense, the walls lined with crystals, tarot cards, and various mystical trinkets. The atmosphere was hushed, as if the very walls held ancient secrets.

"Ah, Jessa and Bryce," a voice called from behind a curtain. Ms. Vesper appeared, her eyes twinkling with an otherworldly wisdom. "I've been expecting you. I could feel the energy shift yesterday."

Bryce and I exchanged a glance, both of us caught

off guard by her foresight. "You knew we were coming?" I asked, incredulous.

Ms. Vesper nodded, a knowing smile playing on her lips. "Indeed. Magic has a way of guiding those who need it to where they must be."

A shiver ran down my spine, the weight of our quest settling in. We were bound by the spell that had brought us here and by the connection that had formed between us—a connection that, despite everything, felt as real and unbreakable as the very magic that had started it all.

bryce

The Arcane Room was unlike any place I'd ever seen. The walls were lined with crystals and trinkets that glimmered under dim lights, casting an otherworldly glow over everything. The air was thick with the intoxicating scent of incense, carrying an almost euphoric energy that made the shop hum with possibilities. It was the kind of place where anything could happen, and I wasn't sure if that excited or terrified me.

Ms. Vesper watched us with a knowing smile, her eyes twinkling with the kind of wisdom that only comes from years of experience in matters far beyond the ordinary.

I exchanged a glance with Jessa, feeling a mix of curiosity and uncertainty. Ms. Vesper motioned for us to sit at a small table draped with a deep purple cloth. As we settled in, her gaze seemed to pierce right through us, as if she could see every thought, every fear, every unspoken word.

"It's not every day that a spell like yours takes effect," she began, her voice soft but filled with an authority that demanded attention. "But when it does, it speaks of desires that run deep and true."

I shifted in my seat, trying to wrap my mind around what she was saying. "What do you mean by that?" I asked, genuinely intrigued but also slightly unnerved.

Ms. Vesper leaned back, folding her hands in her lap, her eyes never leaving ours. "The spell Jessa used only works when the caster is honest about what they truly need in life. It requires more than just words—it demands a piece of your soul."

A piece of your soul. The phrase echoed in my mind, and I found myself glancing at Jessa. She was looking down, her expression contemplative, as if she was trying to piece together the same puzzle. There was a blush creeping up her cheeks, and something about her vulnerability in that moment touched something deep within me. I felt a warmth spreading through my chest, a connection that I hadn't expected but couldn't deny.

"You poured a part of yourself into the spell," Ms. Vesper continued, her eyes locked on Jessa. "And what you asked for was not merely a passing fancy. It was a desire for love and for a connection that transcends time and space."

Jessa's blush deepened, and I couldn't help but feel a surge of protectiveness, an instinct to reach out and comfort her. But I was also caught off guard by the intensity of my own emotions. Was it possible that this crazy, magical mishap had unearthed something I didn't even know I was searching for?

I cleared my throat, trying to regain some semblance of composure. "And what about the other person?" I asked, my voice a bit steadier. "What part do they play in this magic?"

Ms. Vesper turned her gaze to me, her eyes twinkling with a knowing look that made me feel exposed in the best way possible. "The spell would only draw someone who shared those same desires. A person who, whether consciously or not, longs for the same things—a partner who fulfills their soul's need."

Her words hung in the air like a challenge, daring me to confront the truth I'd been avoiding. Deep down, beneath the stoic façade I'd perfected over the years, I'd always yearned for something more than the ordinary. I'd dreamed of a love that defied logic and expectation, a connection that went beyond the mundane.

Jessa and I exchanged a glance, a silent understanding passing between us. The gravity of the situation settled over me like a weight, the realization that we were bound by something far more profound than mere circumstance.

Ms. Vesper's voice broke the silence, pulling us

back to the present. "You must reverse the spell within twenty-four hours, or it will become permanent."

I tensed at the urgency in her words. A quick glance at my watch told me we had only a few hours left. My heart sank at the thought of leaving, but I knew it was the only way to set things right.

"How do we reverse it?" Jessa asked, her voice tinged with resolve, her fingers tightening around the edge of the table.

Ms. Vesper nodded, rising gracefully to gather a few items from around the shop. She returned with a blue candle and a small bag of herbs, handing them to Jessa with the kind of reverence you'd give a sacred relic.

"You'll need to create a simmer pot with these herbs," she explained, her tone steady and assured. "Light the candle, and repeat this incantation together. The spell will begin to unravel, but be warned, the bond you've formed will not simply disappear. It will remain a part of you both."

I took a deep breath, the weight of her words settling in like a bittersweet truth. The bond between us—real and undeniable—would linger, even as we parted ways. The thought was both comforting and heartbreaking.

Ms. Vesper's eyes softened as she looked at us. "Remember, love is the most powerful magic of all. Even if the spell is reversed, its effects may last longer than you realize."

I slipped my hand into Jessa's, feeling her fingers entwine with mine in a gesture that spoke louder than words. It was a silent promise, a commitment to face whatever lay ahead together. She squeezed my hand, and in that moment, I knew we were on the same page, even if we didn't know what the next chapter held.

"Thank you, Ms. Vesper," I said with genuine gratitude.

She smiled, a wise, knowing smile that seemed to carry the weight of lifetimes. "It's been a pleasure, dears. Trust in yourselves and in each other. Magic has a way of leading us to where we truly belong."

As we stood to leave, I felt a pang of sadness at the thought of saying goodbye to this newfound connection. But I also felt a sense of peace, knowing that whatever happened next, we were on the right path.

Jessa and I left The Arcane Room, the door closing softly behind us. The afternoon sun was warm on our faces as we made our way back to her apartment, the world around us seemingly unchanged. Yet inside, everything had shifted.

With the clock ticking down, we had only a few hours left to savor this unexpected adventure and the bond that had formed between us. Despite the inevitable farewell, I couldn't help but feel a sense of hope. Jessa had touched my life in ways I never could have anticipated, and the thought of letting go now seemed impossible.

We walked hand in hand, the warmth of her touch

a constant reminder of what we were fighting for. I couldn't help but wonder what the future had in store for us—for both of us. The magic we'd stumbled into might have been an accident, but the connection we'd found felt like destiny.

"Jessa," I murmured, my voice low and filled with a hunger I could no longer deny. "No matter what happens, I don't regret a single moment of this."

She looked up at me, her eyes wide and filled with the same desire that was coursing through my veins. "Neither do I, Bryce."

With that, I captured her lips in a kiss that was both a promise and a plea—a promise that we would face whatever came next, and a plea that this moment, this connection, would last beyond the spell, beyond time itself. I knew that no matter what magic had brought us together, it was nothing compared to the magic we'd found in each other.

Not now. Not ever.

jessa

The walk back to my apartment felt both endless and all too brief. Each step brought us closer to goodbye—a word that tasted bitter on my tongue. I squeezed Bryce's hand tighter, not ready to let go of the warmth and comfort it provided. My heart ached with the knowledge that soon, he would be gone, back to his own time and place. It was a cruel twist of fate, and I wasn't ready to face it.

We entered my apartment, the space feeling somehow different now—imbued with memories and emotions I hadn't anticipated. The clock ticked softly in the background, a reminder of the precious time slipping away, each second a reminder that we were on borrowed time.

Bryce closed the door behind us and turned to face me, his expression a mix of determination and sadness.

"We don't have much time," he said, his voice gentle yet firm, a painful reminder of the task at hand.

I nodded, though my heart protested. "I know, but —I wish it didn't have to be this way."

His eyes softened, and he stepped closer, brushing a strand of hair from my face. His touch sent shivers down my spine. "Jessa, I want you to know that the past day with you has been more than I could have ever imagined for myself. You've given me something I never thought I'd find—a glimpse of love that feels real."

The sincerity in his words moved through me like a wave, and tears pricked at my eyes. "I don't want you to leave," I admitted, my voice trembling with the weight of the truth. "I didn't expect any of this, but now that you're here, everything else feels wrong."

He cupped my face in his hands, his touch tender and reassuring. "And yet, I must go back. I have responsibilities, a life waiting for me in Scotland. But know this, lass—I've got feelings for you too, feelings I can't ignore."

Bryce's confession filled me with a bittersweet joy. We were two people caught in a whirlwind of magic and fate, destined to part but undeniably connected. I leaned into him, savoring the warmth of his embrace, wanting to hold on to this moment for as long as possible.

We stood like that for a moment, wrapped in silence, each of us silently acknowledging what we had found together. Then, as if sensing the urgency, Bryce leaned in and kissed me—a soft, lingering kiss that conveyed more than words ever could.

As our lips met, the world fell away, leaving only us in a bubble of time suspended between what was and what might be. It was a kiss filled with longing, with the knowledge that this might be our last chance to truly be together.

His hands found my waist, pulling me closer until I was pressed against him, feeling the steady beat of his heart against mine. "Let's not waste what little time we have left," he whispered, his voice low and filled with a promise that sent heat pooling in my belly.

Without another word, he scooped me into his arms, and I laughed softly, the sound wrapping around us like a shared secret. He carried me to the bedroom, where the soft glow of the room set the stage for what was to come.

In the dim light, a sense of intimacy wrapped around us as we took our time undressing each other, savoring every moment, every touch. Bryce's eyes locked onto mine as he reached for the hem of my top, slipping it gently off my shoulders. His fingers brushed against my skin, leaving a trail of tingling warmth in their wake.

He leaned in, his lips following the path of his touch, trailing kisses along the curve of my neck and down to my shoulders. I shivered under his caress, the heat between us building with each passing second, an irresistible pull that defied reason and time.

Bryce's hands moved with deliberate care, tracing the outline of my collarbone before drifting lower, his fingers grazing my breasts. He paused, his gaze darkening with desire as he took one breast into his mouth, his tongue flicking over the sensitive peak with expert precision.

A soft moan escaped my lips as he lavished attention on me, his hands kneading and exploring with a reverence that made my heart race. He moved to the other breast, repeating the motion, and I arched into him, craving more of his touch, more of him.

His kisses trailed lower, down my stomach, each one a promise of what was to come. My body responded eagerly, every nerve alive with anticipation as he knelt before me, spreading my legs with a gentle insistence that left me breathless.

Bryce's eyes met mine, a playful glint dancing in their depths as he lowered his head, his tongue finding my most intimate place. He tasted me with a rhythmic skill that sent waves of pleasure coursing through my body, his touch teasing and precise, driving me wild.

He playfully nipped at my thigh, sending a delicious shiver up my spine before returning to his task, his focus unwavering. The sensation built, a symphony of ecstasy that crescendoed with each flick of his tongue and every whispered sigh, every gasp of my name.

As his expert mouth worked its magic, I felt the tension coil tighter, my breath quickening, heart racing. With a final, exquisite caress, he pushed me over the edge, and I shattered around him, a cry of pure bliss escaping my lips, my body trembling in release.

Before the aftershocks of my orgasm had fully subsided, Bryce rose to his feet, the heat in his gaze matching the fire that burned within me. He entered me slowly, his movements deliberate, a testament to the connection we shared.

We moved together, bodies entwined in a dance, a rhythm that spoke of a love that transcended the boundaries of time. Each thrust felt like a declaration, each caress a reminder of our bond, of what we had discovered in each other.

Bryce explored my body as if committing it to memory. Our breaths mingled in the air, our moans filling the room, a symphony of pleasure that seemed to stretch into eternity. Time stopped, and for a moment, we were suspended together in this perfect, impossible love.

In the aftermath, as our breathing slowed and reality seeped back in, I clung to him, unwilling to let go. The world outside seemed distant, the ticking clock a cruel reminder of what was to come.

Bryce pressed a kiss to my forehead, his touch a soothing balm to the storm inside of me. "It's time," he whispered, his voice filled with a sadness that mirrored my own. I blinked back tears, the thought of losing him tearing at my heart. He wiped away the single tear that fell, his thumb gentle on my cheek. "It's going to be okay, my love."

Reluctantly, we rose from the bed and returned to the living room, where the blue candle and simmer pot awaited. The herbs Ms. Vesper had given us were arranged with care, the incantation ready to be spoken.

We stood together, hand in hand. As we lit the candle, its flame flickered, casting a warm glow that illuminated the room and our faces, a soft reminder of the love we had found.

Bryce squeezed my hand, and I met his gaze, seeing the same mixture of hope and sadness reflected in his eyes. "Let's do this," I said, my voice steady despite the turmoil that churned within me.

Together, we recited the incantation, our voices weaving a tapestry of magic that resonated with the power of our connection. The words flowed like a melody, carrying with them the weight of what was and what could have been.

As the final syllable left our lips, I felt a shift in the air—a gentle tug, as if the universe itself was acknowledging our decision. The room seemed to shimmer, the magic coalescing around us in a vibrant display of light.

I turned to Bryce, tears brimming in my eyes, blurring my vision. "I don't want you to go," I breathed, the words a plea and a farewell wrapped into one, my heart breaking at the thought of losing him.

He smiled, but it didn't reach his eyes. "I'll always remember you, Jessa. You've changed my life in ways I will never have words to explain."

With that, he kissed me—a tender, lingering kiss that held the promise of eternity. And then, as if swept away by the very magic that had brought him to me, Bryce began to fade, his form dissolving into the shimmering light.

In an instant, he was gone, leaving only the echo of his presence and the ache of absence in his wake.

I stood there, the room silent and still, my heart heavy with loss. I curled up on the couch and broke down, sobbing uncontrollably. I couldn't breathe—everything hurt. The spell had been reversed, but the bond lingered, a memory of what I could never have.

The promise of hope had soured in my stomach, threatening to make me sick. It felt like hours had passed as I sat there, caught between the echoes of the past and the emptiness of the present. The silence threatened to overwhelm me, crushing me beneath its weight, when a soft knock sounded at the door.

Hope flared within me, tentative and bright. I rushed to the door, flinging it open.

Bryce stood there, warmth in his eyes, though marked with the subtle changes of time—wrinkles at the corners of his eyes, a maturity that spoke of the years that had passed since we last stood together.

"What? How?" I stammered, disbelief warring with the joy that surged through me. "You just left..."

He smiled, that same irresistible smile that had captured my heart from the very beginning. "I waited," he said simply, stepping forward to close the distance between us. "I waited ten years for you, Jessa. It was the longest ten years of my life, but I knew I had to come back. I couldn't let you think I'd forgotten."

"But how did you find me?" I asked, reaching out to touch his face, needing to confirm that he was real, that this wasn't some cruel trick of the mind.

He chuckled softly, his hand covering mine as he leaned into my touch. "I couldn't remember the name of the town, but I remembered The Arcane Room and Ms. Vesper. So, I called her."

"When?" I whispered, still trying to process the fact that he was standing in front of me.

"Years ago," he replied, his voice filled with the kind of patience and love that only comes from waiting for something you believe in with your whole heart.

I blinked, a wave of understanding washing over me. "That's why she knew your name? You contacted her? Is that why I got the book when I did?"

Bryce nodded, his eyes twinkling with a mixture of amusement and sincerity. "Aye, I think perhaps a part of me was always meant to find you."

His words washed over me, filling the void that had opened in my heart when he'd left. I reached out, tracing the lines of his face, seeing the man he had become—the man who had chosen me, despite the odds, despite the passage of time.

"You came back?" I breathed, emotion choking my voice, the tears that had dried now returning in full force.

He nodded, his gaze steady and filled with love. "I got my visa, just like we talked about. Invested in Byte-Dance, made a life for myself. But it was all for this moment. It was all for you."

Tears spilled down my cheeks, but this time they were tears of joy, of relief. Bryce had returned, against all odds, proving that magic wasn't the only force at play—love was its own kind of magic, a magic that transcended time and space.

He pulled me into his arms, holding me close as if afraid I might vanish if he let go. "I couldn't imagine spending another moment without you," he murmured, pressing a kiss to my hair.

I looked up at him, seeing both the changes and the constants—the wrinkles, the maturity, but also the same twinkle in his eyes, the same warmth in his smile.

"You're still my perfect lover," I whispered, feeling the truth of those words resonate in my soul, grounding me in the reality that this was happening, that he was here, and he wasn't going anywhere.

We stood there, wrapped in each other's arms, the door to the apartment still open, the world outside forgotten. It was a moment of magic and love that felt destined from the start, as if every step we'd taken had led us to this point.

And as we kissed, sealing the promise of a future together, I knew that this was only the beginning.

Not just of our love story, but of a lifetime of moments where time no longer mattered, where the past and future blurred, leaving only the present—the here and now—where Bryce and I belonged.

Together.

epilogue

Jessa
One Year Later

The sun hung low in the sky, casting a golden hue across the rolling hills and the quaint village of Glenmore. The warmth of the Scottish summer enveloped me as I stood on the porch of our cottage, my gaze fixed on Bryce as he worked in the garden. His sleeves were rolled up, revealing strong forearms, and his hair was deliciously tousled by the gentle breeze.

He glanced up, catching my eye, and flashed that

grin that never failed to make my heart flutter—yes, even after all this time. Life in Glenmore was different from Coral Cove, but it was exactly where I wanted to be. The magic of our love had turned this picturesque village into our personal fairy tale.

"Fancy giving me a hand, lass?" Bryce called out, his voice laced with teasing warmth.

I chuckled, making my way down the steps to join him. "Only if you promise not to laugh at my gardening skills. We both know I'm more of a city girl than a green thumb."

He took my hand, pulling me closer until our bodies were flush against each other. His lips brushed my forehead in a soft kiss that sent shivers down my spine. "With you by my side, everything's perfect," he murmured, his eyes locking onto mine with a promise that made my knees weak.

We'd been living in Scotland for nearly nine months now, a decision that felt as natural as breathing. After Bryce returned to my life, we spent weeks catching up on the years we'd lost, savoring every moment as we built a life together that was as vibrant and full of love as the wildflowers in our garden.

Bryce had introduced me to his family, who welcomed me with open arms and an enthusiasm that was both heartwarming and slightly overwhelming. They'd woven me into the fabric of their close-knit community, and before I knew it, Glenmore felt like home. I'd even found a job at the local school, teaching

English to eager young minds who quickly stole a piece of my heart—though not as thoroughly as Bryce had.

Our days were filled with the simple pleasures of life—morning strolls through the village, evenings by the fire, and nights spent tangled in each other's arms. Every day was a new adventure, and every moment was infused with the magic that had brought us together. It was as if the very air we breathed was enchanted, every touch between us sparking a flame that never seemed to dim.

I glanced over at Bryce, who was now tending to a patch of vibrant wildflowers, his touch gentle and sure. Watching him work, I marveled at how seamlessly he'd transitioned into this new chapter of his life, balancing his love for furniture restoration with his commitment to our shared dreams. The man could make a garden grow just by smiling at it.

"So, what do you think?" he asked, gesturing toward the garden with a flourish. "Will these flowers be ready for the harvest festival? Or should we consider them a decorative attempt at best?"

I smiled, admiring the burst of colors that seemed to dance in the sunlight. "They're beautiful, Bryce. Just like everything you do. And if they don't win any prizes, I'm sure we can bribe the judges with your charm."

He laughed, the sound rich and full of life, and before I could react, he'd pulled me into his arms, spinning me around until I was breathless with laughter.

When he finally set me down, he captured my lips in a kiss.

"You're the one who's made everything beautiful, Jessa. I wouldn't have it any other way," he whispered against my lips, his hands still holding me close.

As we stood there, in the warmth of the afternoon, I couldn't help but think about how far we'd come—from a spell gone awry to a love that had surpassed the boundaries of time. It was a story that defied logic, a testament to the power of fate and the magic that resided in every heartbeat. And it was a story that I never wanted to end.

Later that evening, as we sat on the porch, the sky painted with hues of pink and orange, I rested my head on Bryce's shoulder, feeling the steady rise and fall of his chest. It was the most comforting sound in the world, a melody that grounded me in the present moment.

"Do you ever wonder what would've happened if the spell hadn't worked?" I asked, my voice a soft whisper against the tranquil night.

Bryce was silent for a moment, his hand gently stroking my hair in a soothing rhythm. "Sometimes," he admitted, his voice thoughtful and laced with a hint of that Scottish lilt I loved. "But then I realize it doesn't matter. We found each other, Jessa. And that's all that counts."

I felt his words deep in my soul. We were living proof that magic wasn't confined to fairy tales—it was real and tangible, a force that had shaped our lives in the most wondrous ways. A force that had given us the greatest gift of all—each other.

As the stars began to twinkle above, Bryce turned to me, his eyes reflecting the brilliance of the night sky. There was a playful glint in his gaze, the kind that always made me brace myself for whatever mischief he had in mind. "You know, there's something I've been meaning to ask you," he said, his tone light yet serious.

I raised an eyebrow, intrigued by the shift in his demeanor. "Oh? And what might that be? Are you finally going to admit that I'm the better gardener?"

He chuckled, shaking his head. "Not quite, lass. But close." He took my hand, his gaze steady and unwavering, the humor fading into something deeper. "Marry me, Jessa. Make this life we've built official."

My heart skipped a beat, joy bubbling up inside me so fiercely I thought I might float away. The answer was as clear as the constellations that stretched above us.

"Yes," I whispered, tears of happiness glistening in my eyes. "A thousand times, yes."

He pulled me into his arms, lifting me off the ground in a move that made me squeal with laughter, his lips finding mine in a kiss that promised forever. As he set me down, our foreheads resting together, I knew that this was the moment we had been building toward —where magic and love met, creating a bond that would never break.

And as we sat there, wrapped in the embrace of the Scottish night, I knew that our story was just beginning—a tale of love, destiny, and the magic that would continue to guide us through every chapter of our lives. Because with Bryce by my side, I knew that our happily ever after was guaranteed, and every day was a new adventure waiting to unfold.

Sign up for my newsletter and get a free book today!
https://mailchi.mp/158597581671/jax-wilder

If you enjoyed this book be sure to check out my
Tarot Fantasies series:

The Devil's Temptation

DOTTIE:

I never believed in fairy tales, but the moment I stepped into The Arcane Room, I felt a magic I'd always denied myself. Ms. Vesper's velvety voice was a spell of its own. She offered me a chance at the forbidden—all I had to do was draw a tarot card. I drew the Devil card. His name was Lucian, His touch was electric, awakening parts of me I'd kept hidden for so long. I wanted to forget every rule I'd ever made for myself and live in this moment forever.

DOROTHEA HAS ALWAYS PLAYED IT SAFE, HER life confined to the walls of her bakery in the quaint town of Coral Cove. But when she steps into The Arcane Room, an unassuming new age shop, she's thrust into a world where her deepest fantasies come to life. Guided by the enigmatic and dangerously seductive Lucian, Dottie enters a magical experience where her untouched innocence and hidden passions are brought to the surface.

At twenty-nine, Dottie has never experienced the complexities of intimacy. Her untouched innocence is a stark contrast to Lucian's experienced hands. As he guides her through a series of sensually charged encounters, Dottie learns to confront her fears and embrace the desires she's long kept buried. Lucian's dark allure pushes her boundaries, helping her to uncover her inner strength and face the temptations she has always denied herself.

Within the enchanted simulation, Dottie's journey is one of self-discovery and empowerment. In the heart of The Arcane Room, she learns that true strength comes from within, and living fearlessly is the key to unlocking her greatest desires. Through each tantalizing experience, she discovers the courage to embrace her passions and the power to transform her life.

Will Dottie emerge from the magical realm with the confidence to live her life fully, or will her fears continue to hold her back? Enter a world of seduction, secrets, and self-discovery in "The Devil's Temptation," a spellbinding tale that will leave you breathless and yearning for more.

also by jax wilder

Coral Cove Series

Sleighed by Love

Harvesting Love

Dawning Desire

Knead You Now

Love Rewound

Perfect Lover Spell

Tarot Fantasies Series

Devil's Temptation

Strength of the Beast

Death's Embrace

Hanged Passions

Six of Cups

Queen of Pentacles

Additional Books by
Rainbow Quartz Publishing

Lorelai Hamilton:

Teenage Witch's Grimoire

Tarot Reflection Journal

Tarot Refection Journal Coloring The Tarot

The Eclectic Witch's Grimoire

Dream Journal

Teenage Tarot

Tarot Tales and Magic Spells

Arcane In Verse

Find Your Bliss

Miranda Levi: From A Youth A Fountain Did Flow

The Sea Withdrew

A Tear In Time

Mo(ther) Na(ture)

In Orion's Hands

Jackson Anhalt

From The 911 Files

Isla Watts: A Fairy Bad Day

Surprise! You're a Vampire

Gorgeous, Gorgeous, Gorgons

Mork The Handsome Orc

Adopted By Werewolves

Bite Me If You Can

That's The Spirit!

Rose Dawson

Enchanted Escapades

Enchanted Escapades

Dewey Decimal Diaries

Siren's Songbook

Pride and Prejudice

Bibliophile's Bounty

Book of Books Journal

Pages & Passages Reading Journal

Bookworm's Companion Reading Journal & Tracker

about the author

Jax Wilder is a passionate romance author hailing from a charming small town nestled in the picturesque Pacific Northwest. With a heart full of love and an unyielding belief in the power of happily ever afters, Jax weaves enchanting tales of love and connection that leave readers captivated.

Jax's novels are a reflection of her commitment to celebrating the magic of love, and her characters' journeys mirror the warmth and happiness she has found in her own life. Join her on the enchanting journey of love, passion, and enduring connection through her heartfelt romance novels.

Sign up for my newsletter and get a free book today!

https://mailchi.mp/158597581671/jax-wilder